# Dear Parent:
## Your child's love of reading starts here!

Every child learns to read in a different way and at his or her own speed. You can help your young reader improve and become more confident by encouraging his or her own interests and abilities. You can also guide your child's spiritual development by reading stories with biblical values and Bible stories, like I Can Read! books published by Zonderkidz. From books your child reads with you to the first books he or she reads alone, there are I Can Read! books for every stage of reading:

**SHARED READING**
Basic language, word repetition, and whimsical illustrations, ideal for sharing with your emergent reader.

**BEGINNING READING**
Short sentences, familiar words, and simple concepts for children eager to read on their own.

**READING WITH HELP**
Engaging stories, longer sentences, and language play for developing readers.

**READING ALONE**
Complex plots, challenging vocabulary, and high-interest topics for the independent reader.

**ADVANCED READING**
Short paragraphs, chapters, and exciting themes for the perfect bridge to chapter books.

I Can Read! books have introduced children to the joy of reading since 1957. Featuring award-winning authors and illustrators and a fabulous cast of beloved characters, I Can Read! books set the standard for beginning readers.

A lifetime of discovery begins with the magical words "I Can Read!"

Visit www.icanread.com for information on enriching your child's reading experience.
Visit www.zonderkidz.com for more Zonderkidz I Can Read! titles.

"None of you should look out just for
your own good. You should also look out
for the good of others."
— Philippians 2:4

ZONDERKIDZ

*Knights, Vikings, and a Battle of the Bands*
Copyright © 2012 by Big Idea, Inc. VEGGIETALES.® character names, likenesses and
other indicia are trademarks of Big Idea, Inc. All rights reserved.

Requests for information should be addressed to:

Zonderkidz, 5300 Patterson Ave SE, Grand Rapids, Michigan 49530

ISBN 978-0-310-74203-6

Princess Petunia and the Good Knight ISBN 9780310732068
Whats Up with Lyle ISBN 9780310727323
Junior Battles to Be His Best ISBN 9780310721604

*Editor: Mary Hassinger*
*Art Direction: Diane Mielke*

*Printed in China*

13  14  15  16 /DSC/ 22  21  20  19  18  17  16  15  14  13  12  11  10  9  8  7  6  5  4  3  2  1

# I Can Read!

BEGINNING 1 READING

# Princess Petunia and the Good Knight

story by Karen Poth

The Castle of Scone

was a busy place!

Everyone came to see

the Great Pie Games!

Music played!

The Peas sang!

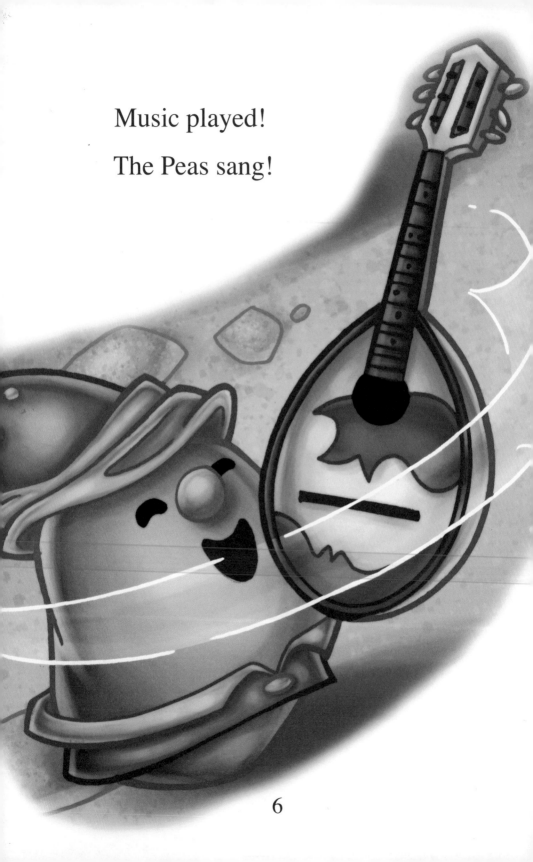

All the Veggies were happy!
They waited for the games
to start.

Princess Petunia looked
down at the field.
She saw a table piled
with fresh, sticky pies.
There were many brave men
waiting to play!

As the pie games began,

pies flew everywhere.

Bump in the Knight won!

"I am the greatest!" he said.

He was bragging.

He was not a very nice knight.

The crowd cheered for the winner.
The Duke of Scone went to help
the knight who lost.

Princess Petunia watched the Duke.

"That is very nice," she thought.

Then the announcer said,

"Next will be the game between

Saturday Knight and Late Knight."

The crowd cheered.

Saturday Knight brushed his hair!

When the Late Knight arrived,

pies flew again!

There was chocolate, banana, apple …

Saturday Knight was creamed!

His hair was a mess!

The Duke helped Saturday Knight.

The Princess watched and smiled.

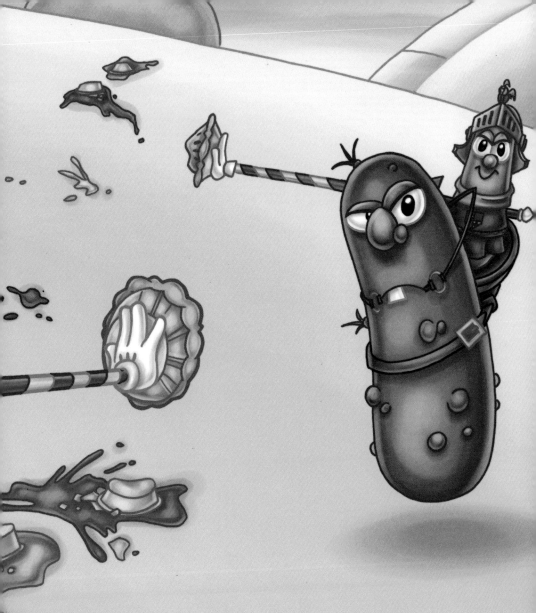

Then, it was the Duke's turn to play.

He had to face the meanest knight of all …

Stormy Knight!

As the two knights took aim,

the Duke heard

a cry from the crowd.

"Mommy!"

The Duke was worried.

He turned to look.

# Ka-Pow!

The Duke of Scone was creamed!

But he wasn't sad.

He ran into the seats to

help the lost child.

At the end of the day,

the winner would be named

by one of the fair maidens.

The Queen of Scone tossed some flowers.

Petunia caught them.

SHE would name the big winner!

Petunia walked down to the field.

All the knights were there.

"I choose the Duke of Scone," she said.

"He is the winner!"

All the other knights were mad.

"But Princess," Duke said.

"I lost the pie game!"

"No," said Petunia.

"By helping all the others,

You are a WINNER!"

"Duke of Scone," the queen said,

"for putting others before yourself,

you have won the Great Pie Games!"

Don't be proud at all. Be completely gentle. Be patient. Put up with one another in love.
— Ephesians 4:2

# What's Up with Lyle?

story by Karen Poth

A long time ago,

in a faraway place,

there lived a group of Vikings.

Do you know who the

Vikings were?

Vikings were sailors.

They rode in big ships.

Vikings ate funny food.

They wore furry hats.

Some hats had two horns.

Some hats had one horn.

Some hats had no horns at all!

Most Vikings were mean!
Everyone was scared of
the Vikings.

They were always frowning.

They picked fights with

other Vikings.

They NEVER made their beds.

But this group of Vikings
was not like all the others.
They lived on Noble Island.
They were very nice.

These Vikings NEVER frowned.

They sang a lot of funny songs.

They ALWAYS made their beds.

One day, mean Vikings

came to Noble Island.

"Come with us," Ugalee yelled.

"We are going to rob the monks!"

"We can't come today,"

Sven said.

"We are going to the fair!"

"The fair?" Ugalee laughed.

"You are a Viking!

Vikings do not go to the fair!"

Ugalee was mad at the nice Vikings.

"I will teach them a lesson,"

he said.

Ugalee left Noble Island.

As soon as Ugalee was gone,

Lyle, a young Viking from

the village, stopped by.

"Hi, guys," Lyle said.

"Where are you going?"

"We are going to the fair," Sven said.

"Would you like to come along?"

"Sure!" Lyle answered.

"I will bring my knitting."

Lyle was not like the rest

of the Vikings.

He did not really like

to sail or fish.

Lyle liked to knit.

The Vikings laughed at Lyle.

That hurt his feelings.

On the way to the fair,

Lyle sat by himself on the ship.

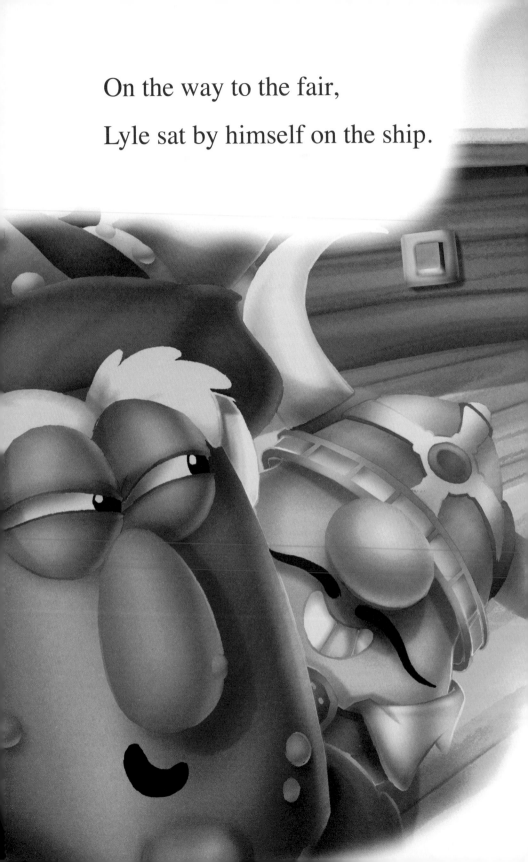

The nice Vikings WERE NOT

being nice at all!

But when they reached the fair

all the Vikings had a lot of fun.

Even Lyle!

They played Viking games.

They ate Viking food.

They even swam in the

Viking pool!

Until …

It started to rain.

"Get to the ship!"

the captain yelled.

A huge storm was coming.

The Vikings had to get home.

Sven and his friends ran to the ship.

But there was a BIG problem.

Ugalee and his crew were there.

They had torn the sails.

They had broken the oars.

"We will never get home!"

Ottar cried.

"The sails won't work with holes!

And we cannot row with

broken oars."

"Do not worry," Lyle smiled.

"I know a way!"

He quickly got to work

knitting patches for the sails.

In no time at all

Lyle had fixed the sails.

Lyle saved the day!

The ship sailed back to

Noble Island.

"I'm sorry, Lyle," Sven said.

"We were mean because

you are different."

"And if you weren't different,
we would not have gotten home,"
the captain said.

"Three cheers for Lyle!"

Don't be proud at all. Be
completely gentle. Be patient.
Put up with one another in love.

— Ephesians 4:2

... For the LORD will be at your side
and will keep your foot from being snared.
—Proverbs 3:26

# I Can Read!

BEGINNING
1
READING

# Junior Battles to Be His Best

story by Karen Poth

Junior's dad was reading the newspaper.

"Junior," he said, "here's a story about

the Bumblyburg Battle of the Bands!"

"You and your friends should enter,"
Dad said.

"No, Dad," Junior said. "I don't want to
play my tuba. Everyone will laugh at me."

Junior's mom convinced him to try.

"You just have to practice," Mom said.

"You'll see. A little hard work

will pay off!"

Junior tried. But he got frustrated.

"It's too hard," Junior said.

"I'm not going to do it."

The next day,

Jimmy and Jerry saw the

Battle of the Bands poster.

They found Junior at The Hop.

Jimmy and Jerry asked Junior to help
get a band together.

"No," Junior said.

"I'm not going to do it.

It's just too hard."

Jimmy and Jerry were sad.
But they decided to do it
even if Junior wouldn't help.

All the next week,
Junior saw his friends practicing
with their bands.

On Monday, he saw Jenny Gourd's band,

The Bubblegum Pop Rockers.

They practiced at the playground.

On Tuesday, Junior saw

Larry and the Peas.

Their band was called Heavy Metal.

Larry was the drummer.

He looked so cool!

On Wednesday, Junior heard

Pa Grape's band, The Space Cadets.

They sounded pretty good.

But they looked a little funny.

Junior started to feel left out.

Then Junior saw Ma Mushroom.

"Are you playing in the battle?" Ma asked.

"No," Junior said. "I'm not good enough."

Ma Mushroom smiled.

"Good," she said. "Then we'll win for sure!

It sounds like you already beat yourself!"

"What do you mean?" Junior asked.

"Well, if you don't try,

then you've already lost," Ma said.

Junior felt terrible.

Ma Mushroom was right.

He had not even tried.

When Junior got home

he practiced his tuba.

And he practiced some more …

"Junior," his mom said, "you are really
sounding great! Maybe next year you'll
enter the battle of the bands!"

"No, Mom," Junior said.

"I don't think I'm good enough."

"Why don't you pray about it?" Mom said.

That night, Junior asked God

to give him courage to play

in front of others some day!

Finally, it was Saturday,

the day of the big battle.

The whole town was there.

Everyone played very well.

In the end only two bands were left—

Jimmy and Jerry's Blues Band

and Ma Mushroom's Swingers!

"We have a tie!" the judge said.

"You will each play one more song.

Give it ALL you've got!"

Jimmy ran out in the audience.

He found Junior.

"Junior, we need you," Jimmy said.

Junior jumped up with a smile.

He went to the stage.

He played his best.

It was just what the Blues Band needed.

Jimmy and Jerry's Blues Band won!

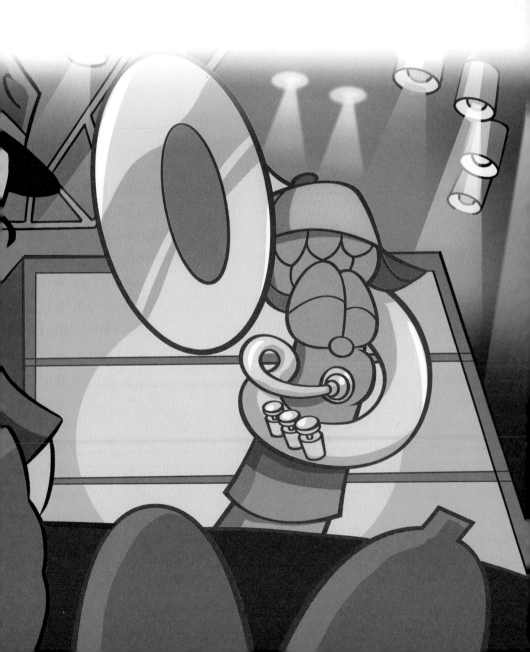

And so did Junior!

"Thank you for your help, God!"

Junior prayed.